VADER: VOLUME 3

Turmoil has engulfed the Galactic Empire. After the destruction of THE DEATH STAR, the disgraced Sith Lord, DARTH VADER, has been demoted by his Master only to have his control be taken by Grand General Tagge. And when Vader discovered that a mole has been leaking information to pirate raiders, it was made clear to him that no person can be trusted.

Unknown to Emperor Palpatine and Tagge, however, Vader is also quietly pursuing his own interests: the mysterious Force-strong pilot who destroyed the Death Star and the identity of the stranger who is conspiring with the Emperor.

But for this he will need his own personal, secret forces....

KIERON GILLEN
Writer

SALVADOR LARROCA
Artist

EDGAR DELGADO
Colorist

VC's JOE CARAMAGNA
Letterer

ADI GRANOV
Cover Artist

HEATHER ANTOS &
CHARLES BEACHAM
Assistant Editors

JORDAN D. WHITE
Editor

C.B. CEBULSKI &
MIKE MARTS
Executive Editors

AXEL
ALONSO
Editor In Chief

JOE
QUESADA
Chief Creative Officer

DAN
BUCKLEY
Publisher

For Lucasfilm:
Senior Editor JENNIFER HEDDLE
Creative Director MICHAEL SIGLAIN
Lucasfilm Story Group RAYNE ROBERTS, PABLO HIDALGO,
LELAND CHEE

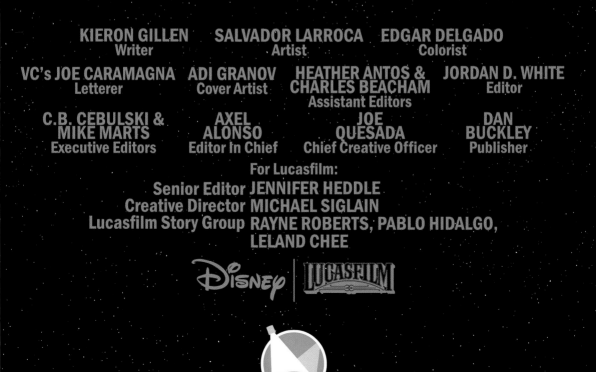

DISNEP | LUCASFILM

ABDOPUBLISHING.COM

Reinforced library bound edition published in 2017 by Spotlight,
a division of ABDO, PO Box 398166, Minneapolis, Minnesota 55439.
Spotlight produces high-quality reinforced library bound editions for
schools and libraries. Published by agreement with Marvel Characters, Inc.

Printed in the United States of America, North Mankato, Minnesota.
042016
092016

THIS BOOK CONTAINS
RECYCLED MATERIALS

STAR WARS © & TM 2016 LUCASFILM LTD.

PUBLISHER'S CATALOGING IN PUBLICATION DATA

Names: Gillen, Kieron, author. | Larroca, Salvador ; Delgado, Edgar, illustrators.
Title: Vader / by Kieron Gillen ; illustrated by Salvador Larroca and Edgar Delgado.
Description: Minneapolis, MN : Spotlight, [2017] | Series: Star Wars : Darth Vader
Summary: Follow Vader straight from the ending of A New Hope into his own solo
adventures-showing the Empire's war with the Rebel Alliance from the other
side! When the Dark Lord needs help, to whom can he turn?
Identifiers: LCCN 2016932362 | ISBN 9781614795209 (v.1 : lib. bdg.) | ISBN
9781614795216 (v. 2 : lib. bdg.) | ISBN 9781614795223 (v. 3 : lib. bdg.) | ISBN
9781614795230 (v. 4 : lib. bdg.) | ISBN 9781614795247 (v.5 : lib. bdg.) | ISBN
9781614795254 (v. 6 : lib. bdg.)
Subjects: LCSH: Vader, Darth (Fictitious character)--Juvenile fiction. | Star Wars
fiction--Comic books, strips, etc.--Juvenile fiction. | Graphic novels--Juvenile
fiction.
Classification: DDC 741.5--dc23
LC record available at http://lccn.loc.gov/2016932362

Spotlight

A Division of ABDO
abdopublishing.com

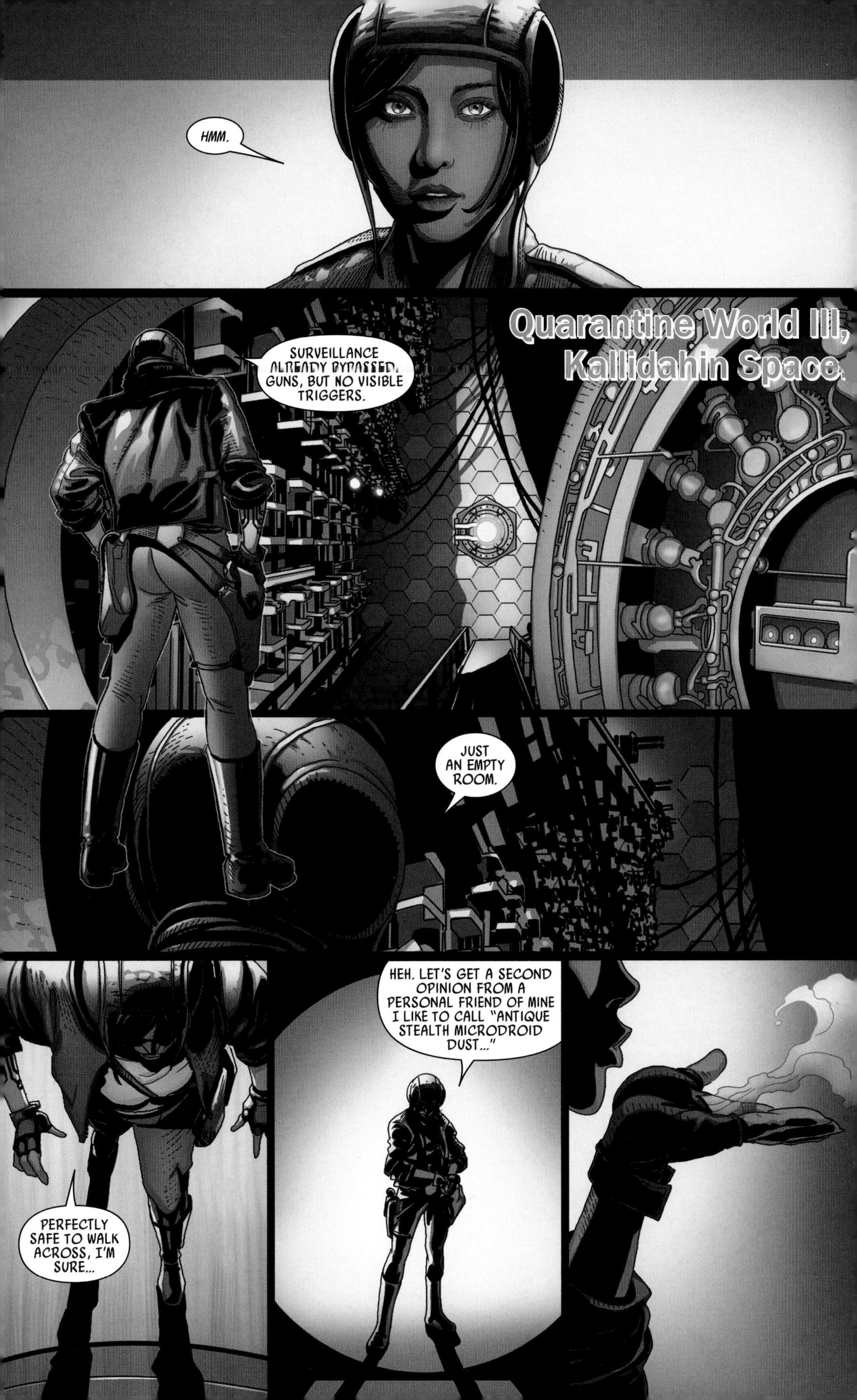
HMM.
Quarantine World III, Kallidahin Space.
SURVEILLANCE ALREADY BYPASSED. GUNS, BUT NO VISIBLE TRIGGERS.
JUST AN EMPTY ROOM.
PERFECTLY SAFE TO WALK ACROSS, I'M SURE...
HEH. LET'S GET A SECOND OPINION FROM A PERSONAL FRIEND OF MINE I LIKE TO CALL "ANTIQUE STEALTH MICRODROID DUST..."

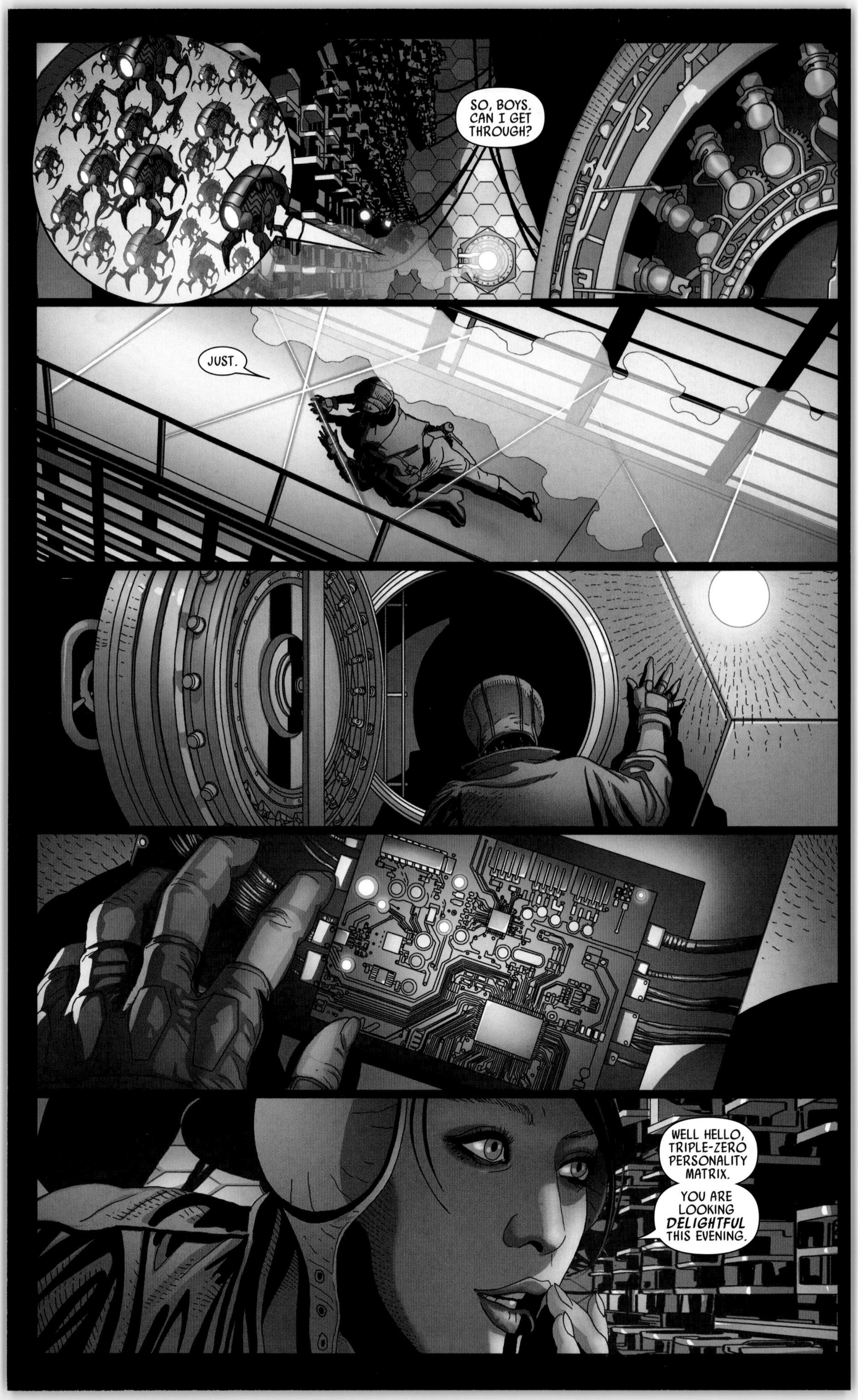
SO, BOYS. CAN I GET THROUGH?
JUST.
WELL HELLO, TRIPLE-ZERO PERSONALITY MATRIX.
YOU ARE LOOKING *DELIGHTFUL* THIS EVENING.

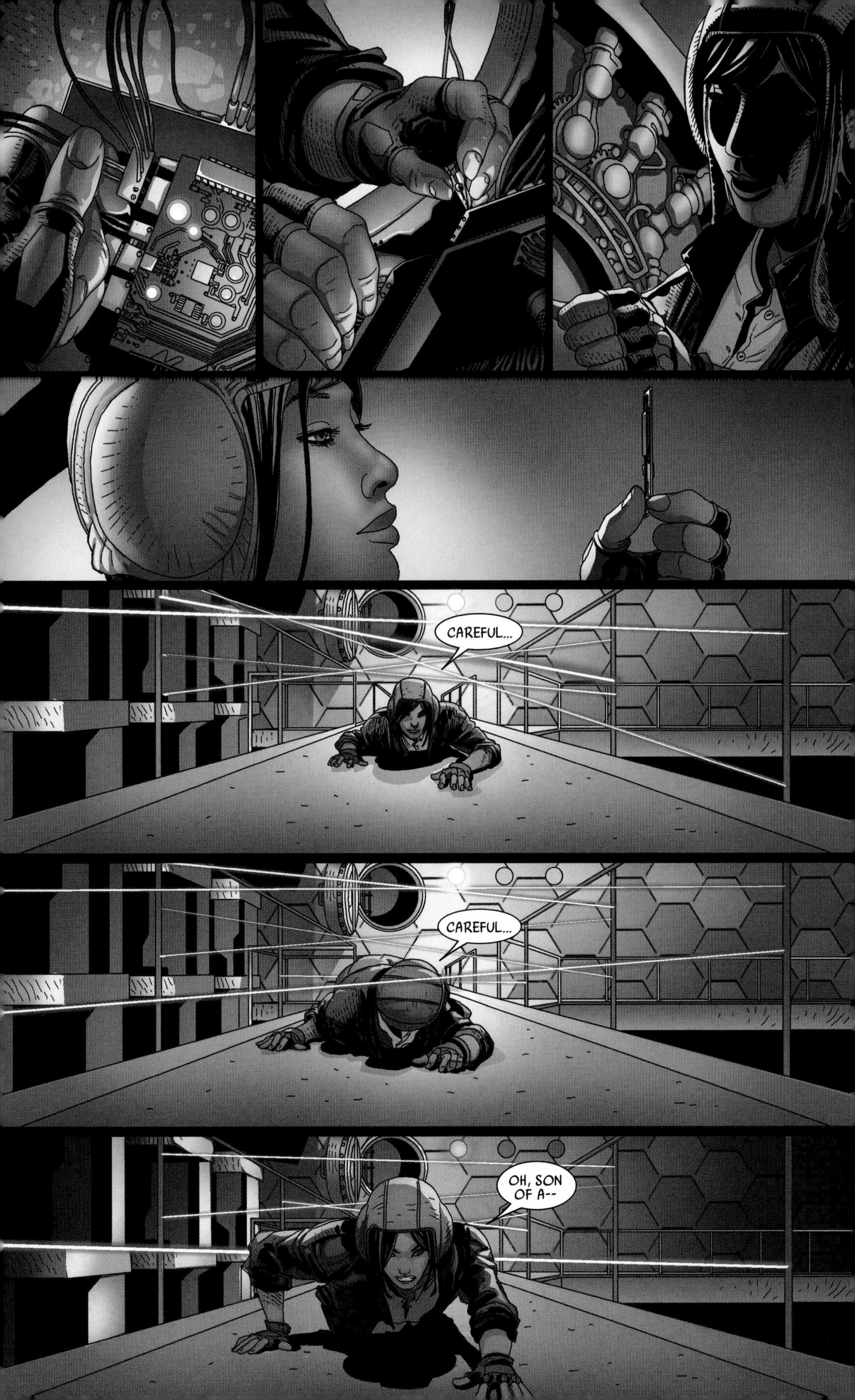
CAREFUL...
CAREFUL...
OH, SON OF A--

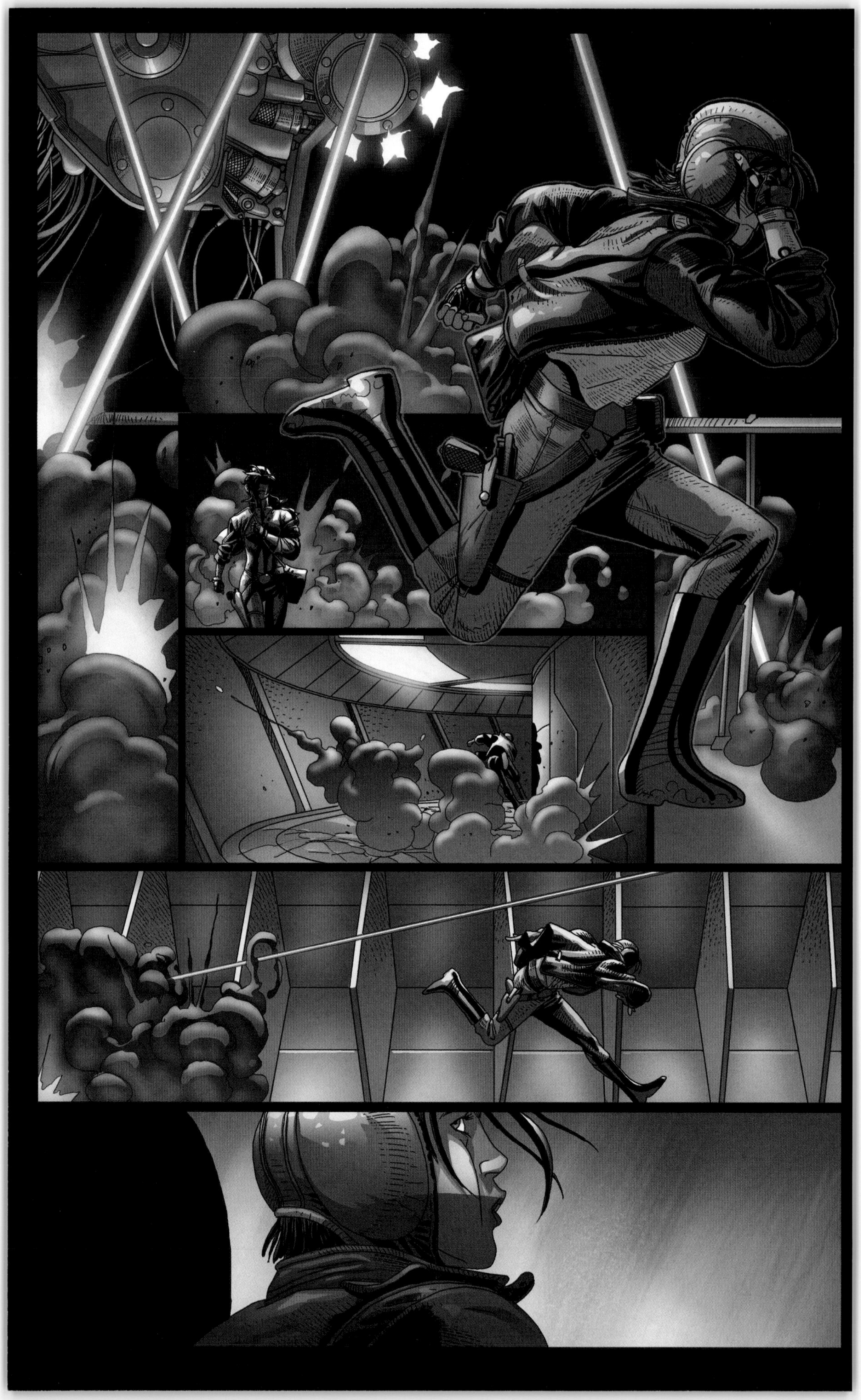

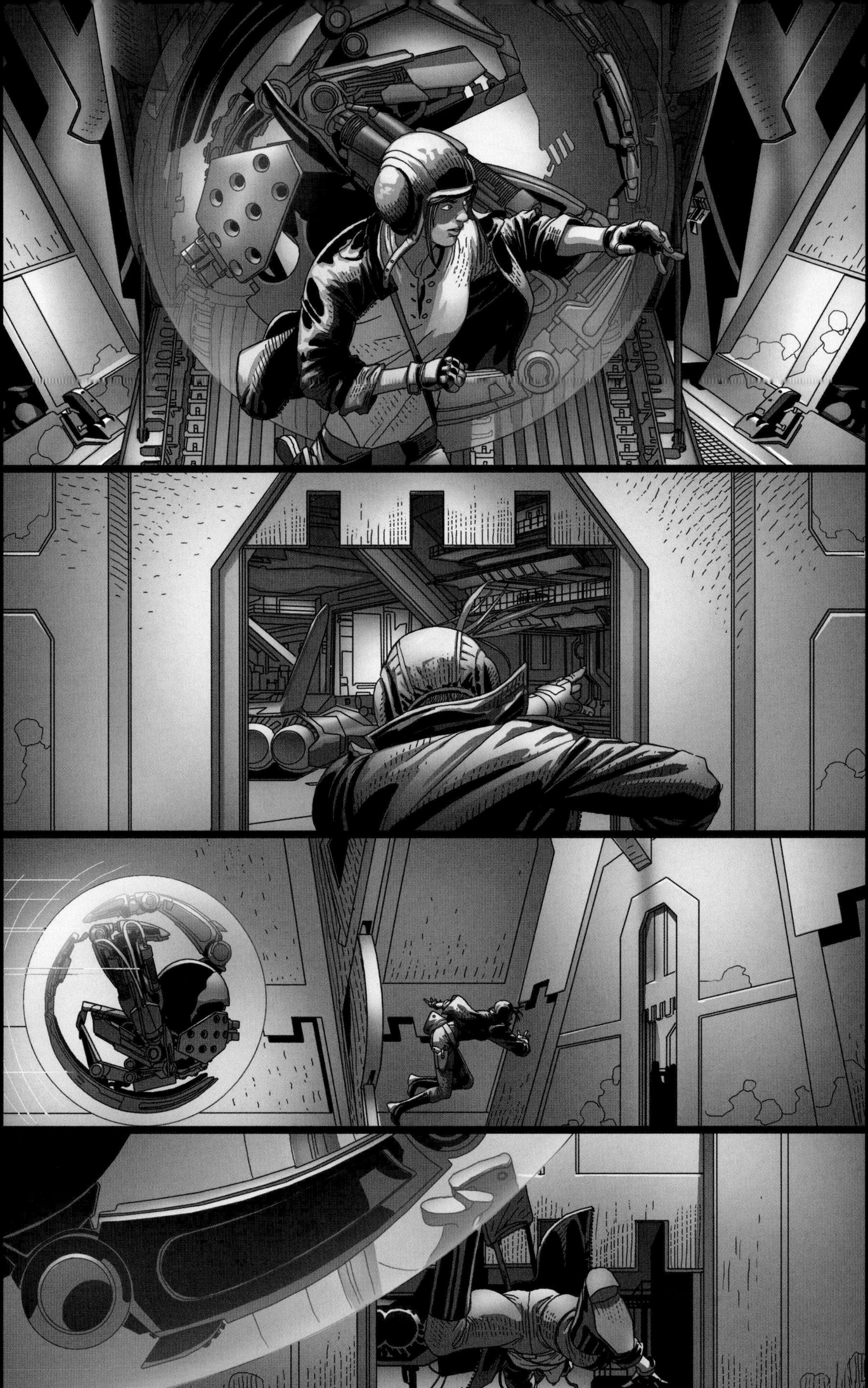

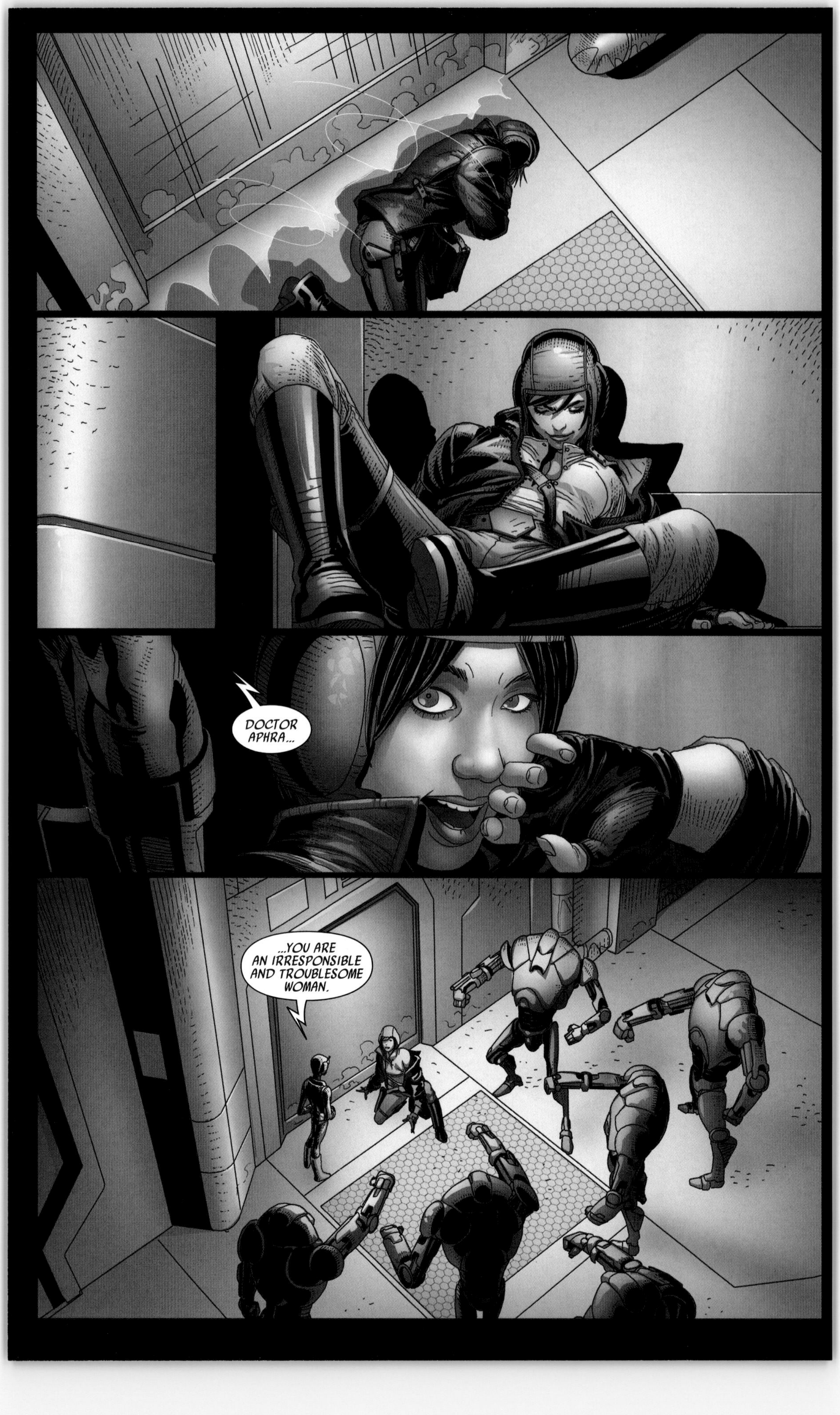
DOCTOR APHRA...
...YOU ARE AN IRRESPONSIBLE AND TROUBLESOME WOMAN.

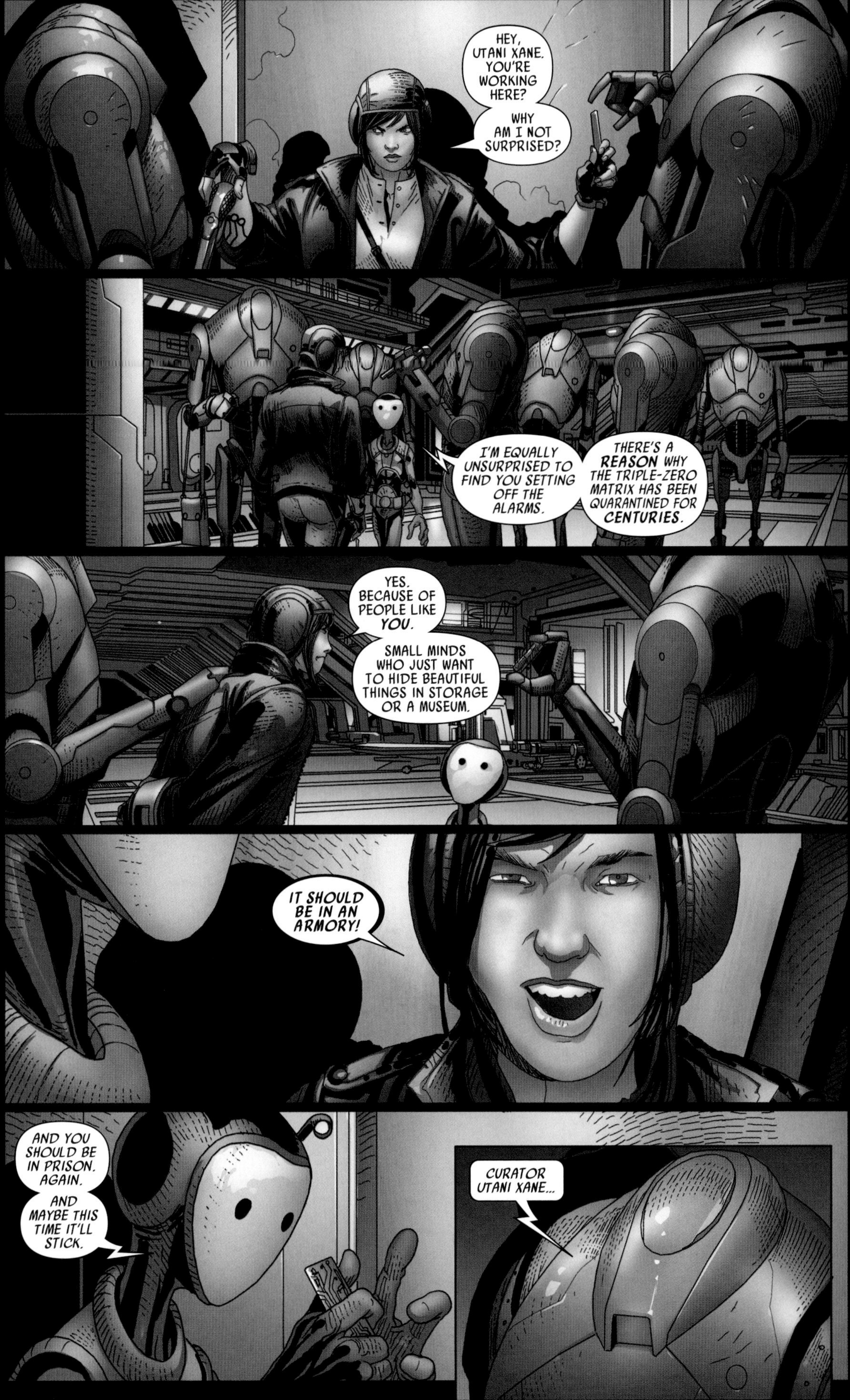
HEY, UTANI XANE. YOU'RE WORKING HERE?
WHY AM I NOT SURPRISED?
I'M EQUALLY UNSURPRISED TO FIND YOU SETTING OFF THE ALARMS.
THERE'S A REASON WHY THE TRIPLE-ZERO MATRIX HAS BEEN QUARANTINED FOR CENTURIES.
YES. BECAUSE OF PEOPLE LIKE YOU.
SMALL MINDS WHO JUST WANT TO HIDE BEAUTIFUL THINGS IN STORAGE OR A MUSEUM.
IT SHOULD BE IN AN ARMORY!
AND YOU SHOULD BE IN PRISON. AGAIN.
AND MAYBE THIS TIME IT'LL STICK.
CURATOR UTANI XANE...

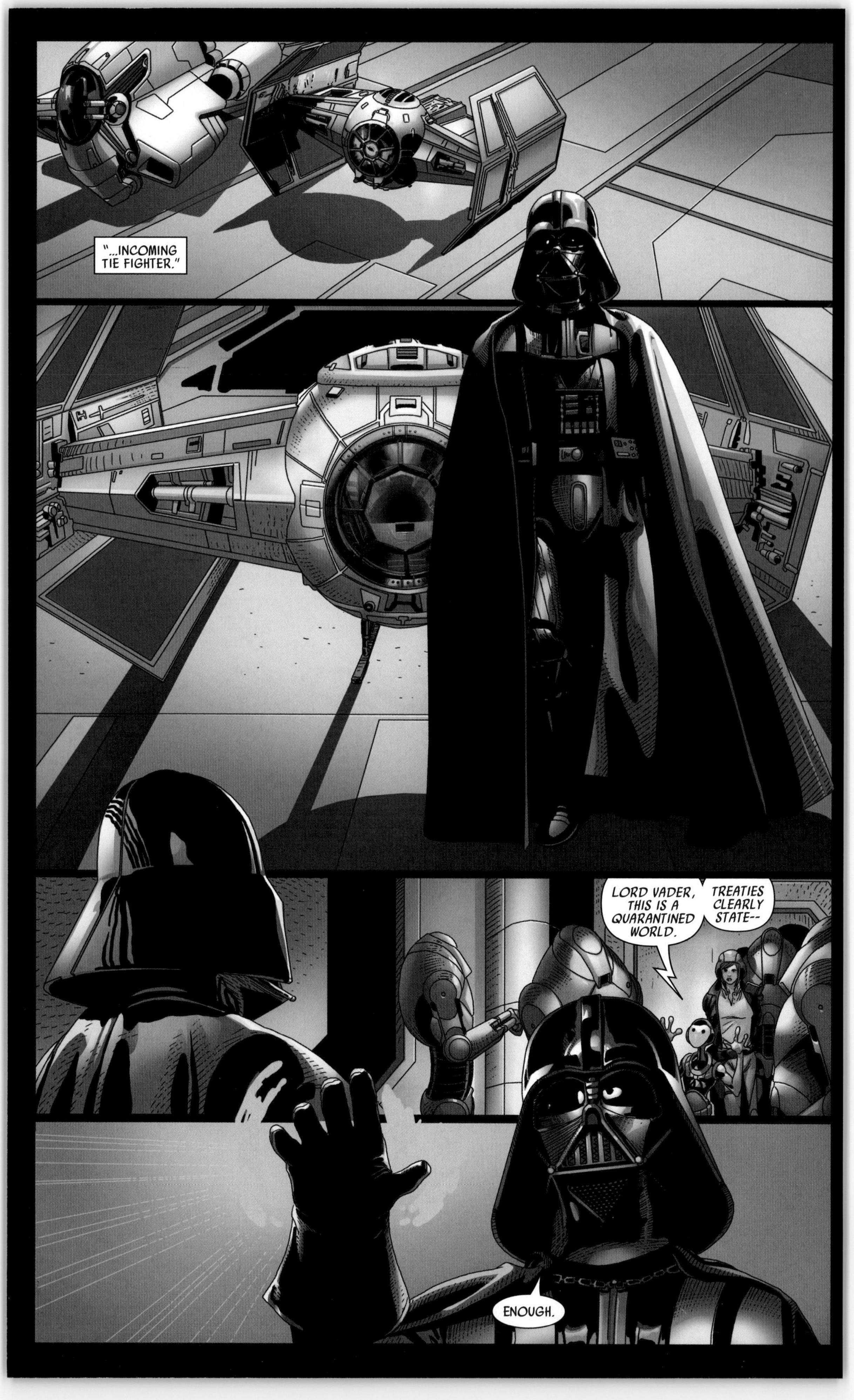
"...INCOMING TIE FIGHTER."
LORD VADER, THIS IS A QUARANTINED WORLD.
TREATIES CLEARLY STATE--
ENOUGH.

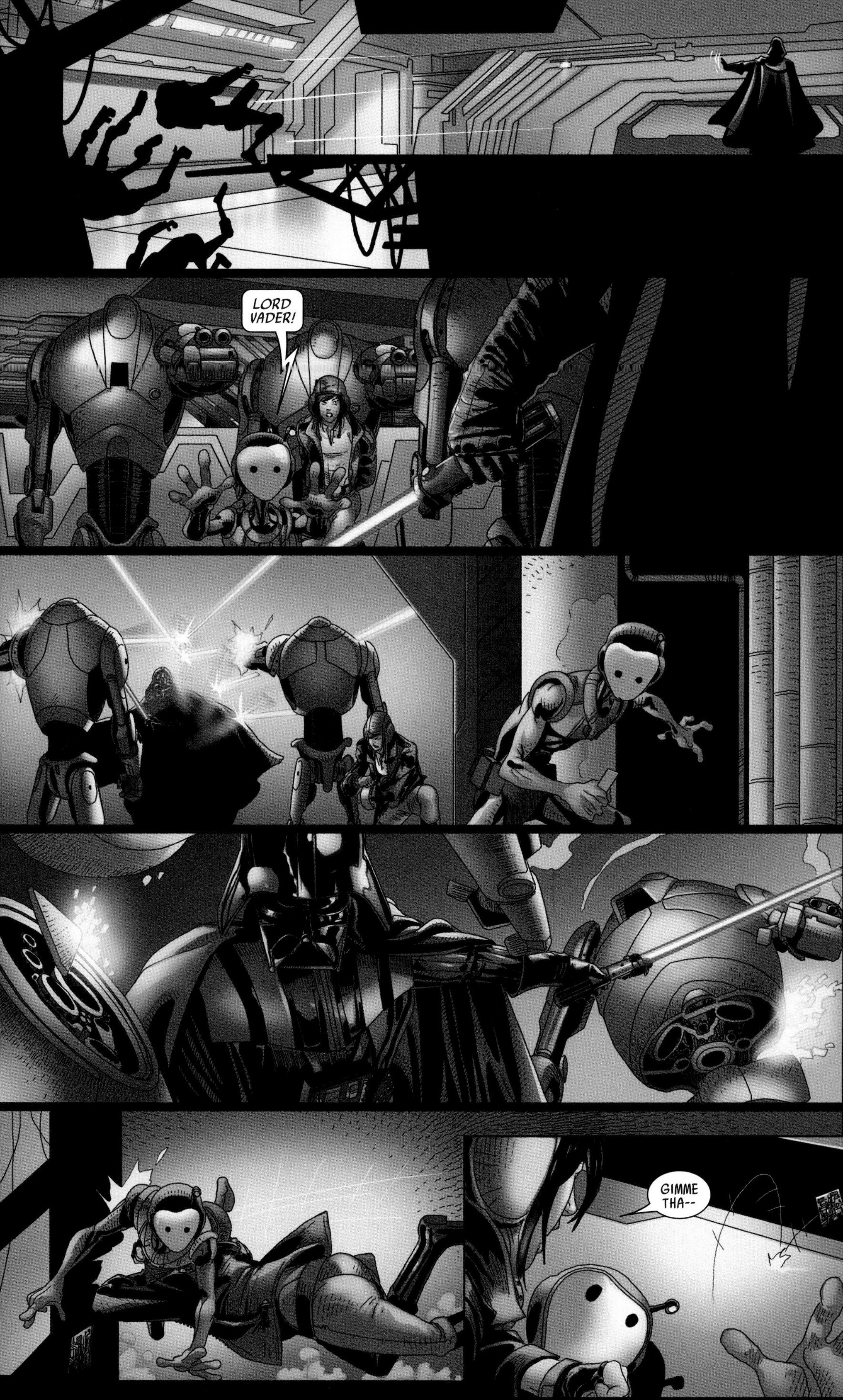
LORD VADER!
GIMME THA--

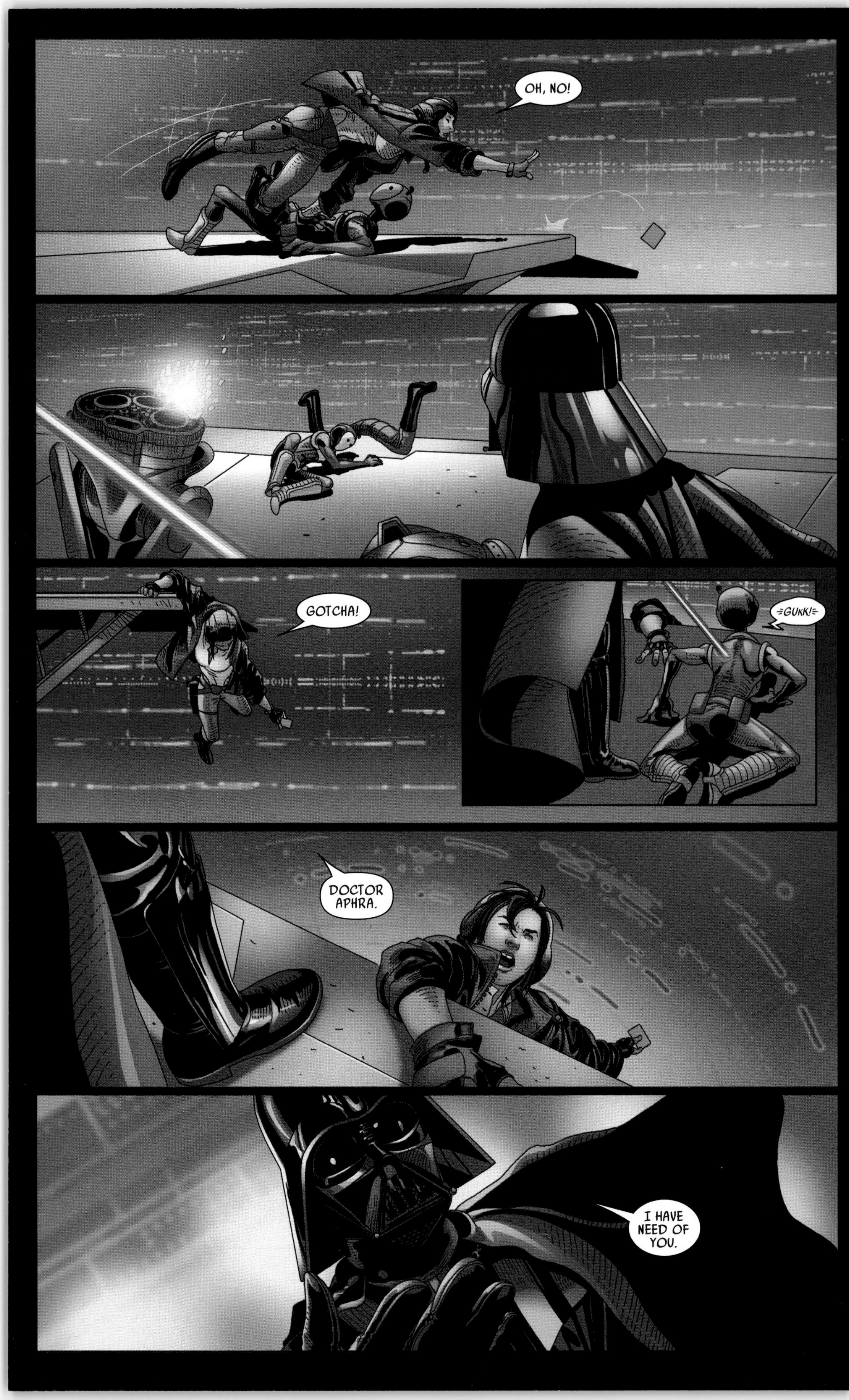
OH, NO!
GOTCHA!
=GUKK!=
DOCTOR APHRA.
I HAVE NEED OF YOU.

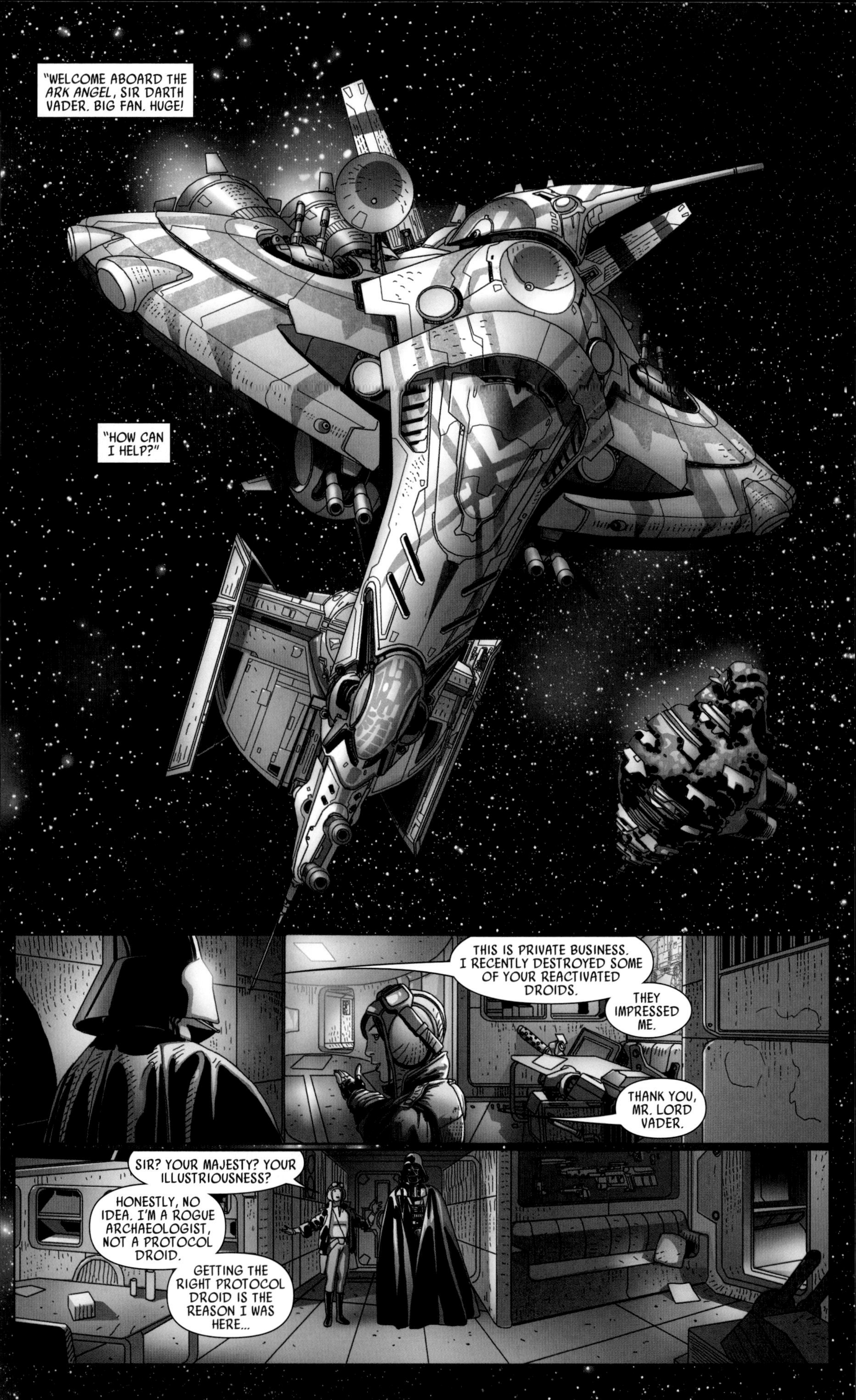
"WELCOME ABOARD THE ARK ANGEL, SIR DARTH VADER. BIG FAN. HUGE!
"HOW CAN I HELP?"
THIS IS PRIVATE BUSINESS. I RECENTLY DESTROYED SOME OF YOUR REACTIVATED DROIDS.
THEY IMPRESSED ME.
THANK YOU, MR. LORD VADER.
SIR? YOUR MAJESTY? YOUR ILLUSTRIOUSNESS?
HONESTLY, NO IDEA. I'M A ROGUE ARCHAEOLOGIST, NOT A PROTOCOL DROID.
GETTING THE RIGHT PROTOCOL DROID IS THE REASON I WAS HERE...

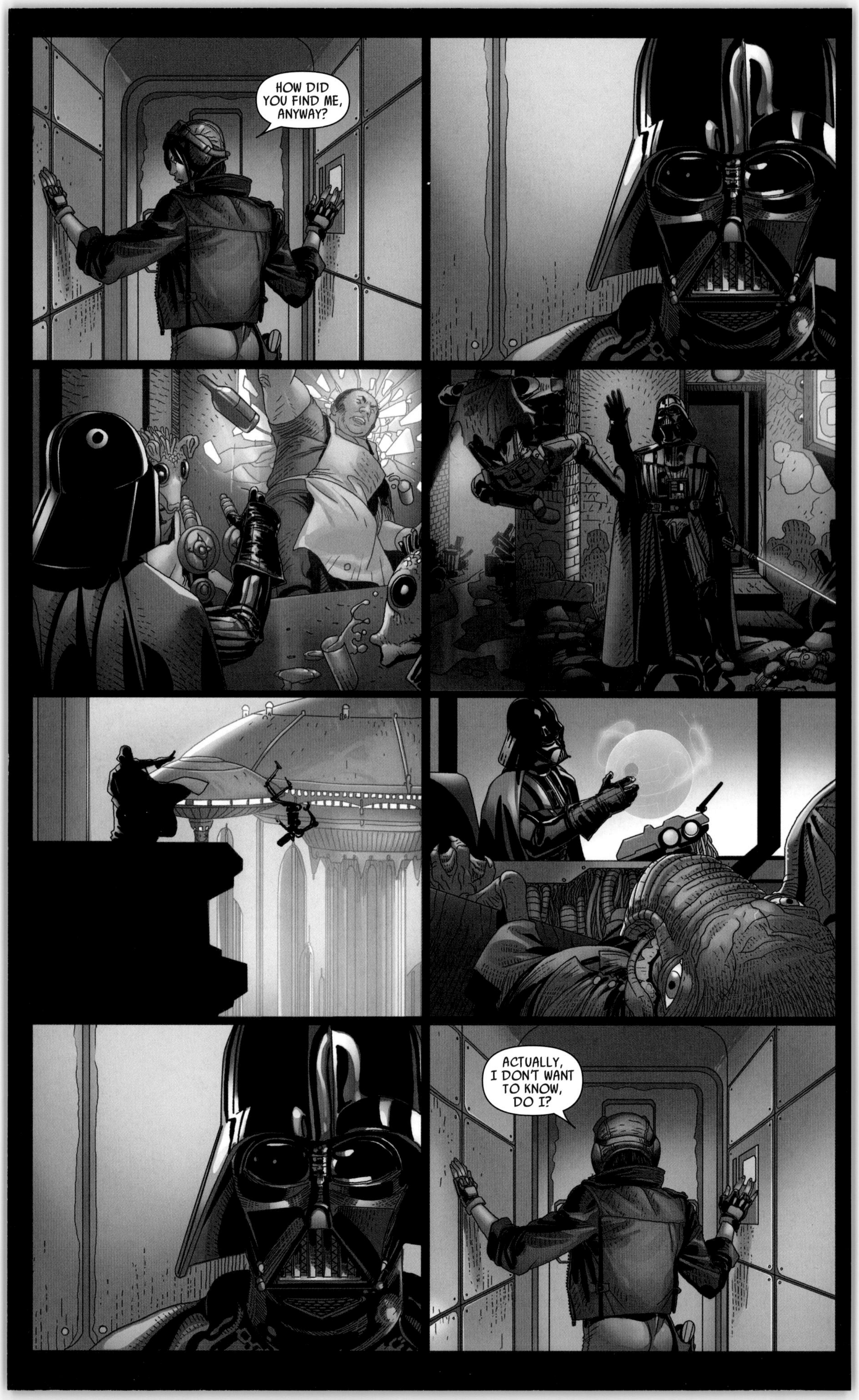
HOW DID YOU FIND ME, ANYWAY?
ACTUALLY, I DON'T WANT TO KNOW, DO I?

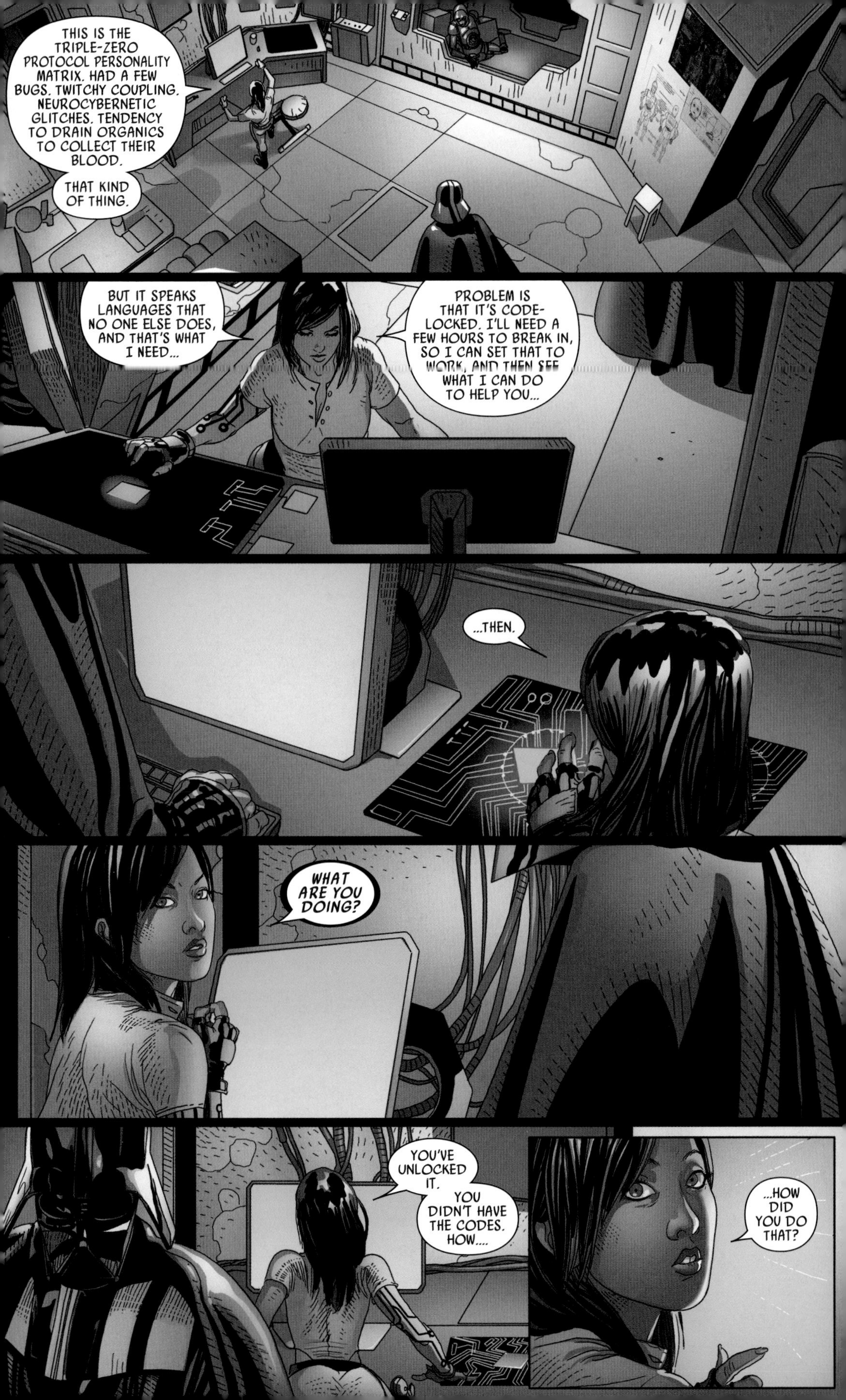

THIS IS THE TRIPLE-ZERO PROTOCOL PERSONALITY MATRIX. HAD A FEW BUGS. TWITCHY COUPLING. NEUROCYBERNETIC GLITCHES. TENDENCY TO DRAIN ORGANICS TO COLLECT THEIR BLOOD.
THAT KIND OF THING.
BUT IT SPEAKS LANGUAGES THAT NO ONE ELSE DOES, AND THAT'S WHAT I NEED...
PROBLEM IS THAT IT'S CODE-LOCKED. I'LL NEED A FEW HOURS TO BREAK IN, SO I CAN SET THAT TO WORK, AND THEN SEE WHAT I CAN DO TO HELP YOU...
...THEN.
WHAT ARE YOU DOING?
YOU'VE UNLOCKED IT.
YOU DIDN'T HAVE THE CODES. HOW....
...HOW DID YOU DO THAT?

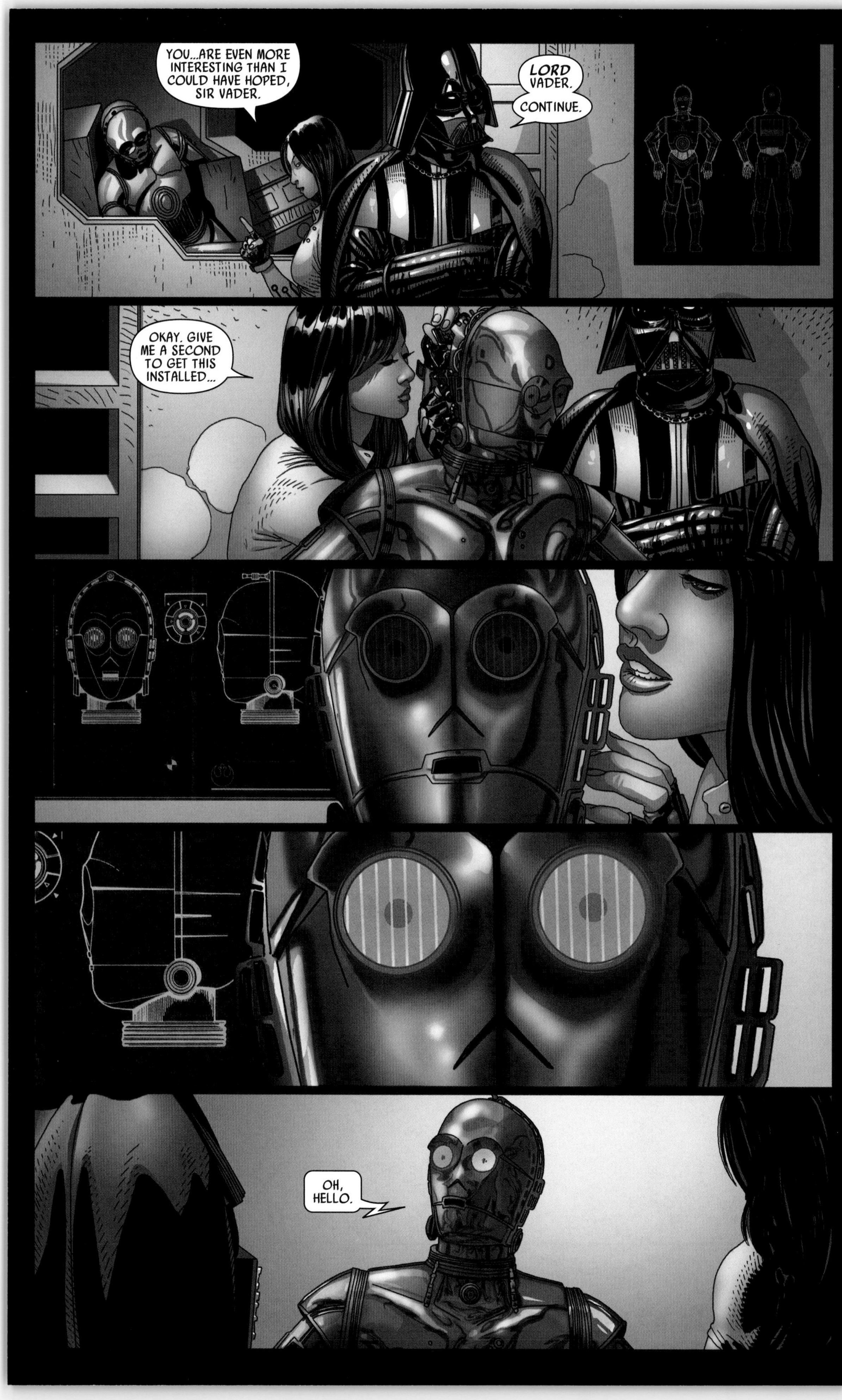
YOU...ARE EVEN MORE INTERESTING THAN I COULD HAVE HOPED, SIR VADER.
LORD VADER.
CONTINUE.
OKAY. GIVE ME A SECOND TO GET THIS INSTALLED...
OH, HELLO.

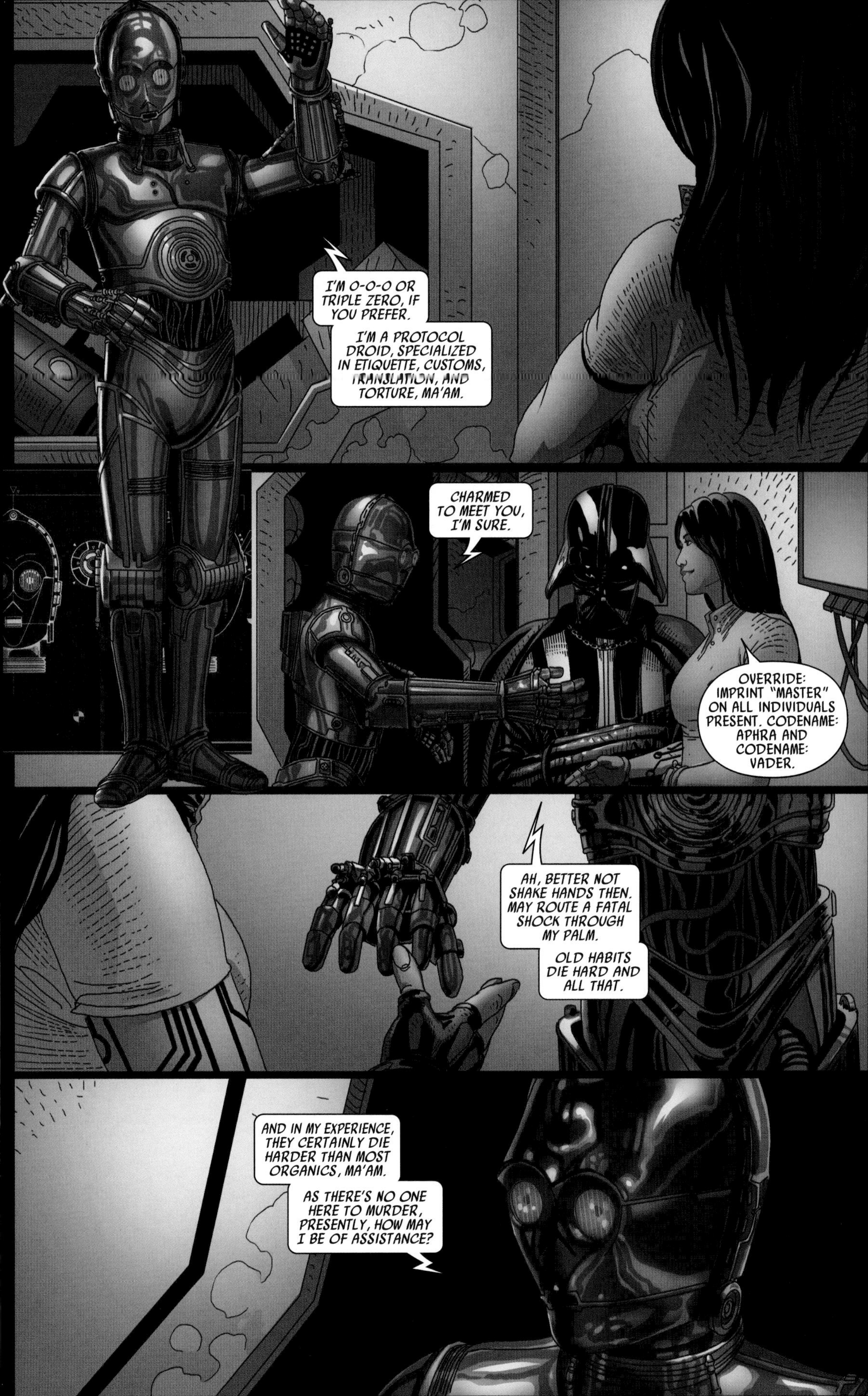
I'M 0-0-0 OR TRIPLE ZERO, IF YOU PREFER.
I'M A PROTOCOL DROID, SPECIALIZED IN ETIQUETTE, CUSTOMS, TRANSLATION, AND TORTURE, MA'AM.
CHARMED TO MEET YOU, I'M SURE.
OVERRIDE: IMPRINT "MASTER" ON ALL INDIVIDUALS PRESENT. CODENAME: APHRA AND CODENAME: VADER.
AH, BETTER NOT SHAKE HANDS THEN. MAY ROUTE A FATAL SHOCK THROUGH MY PALM.
OLD HABITS DIE HARD AND ALL THAT.
AND IN MY EXPERIENCE, THEY CERTAINLY DIE HARDER THAN MOST ORGANICS, MA'AM.
AS THERE'S NO ONE HERE TO MURDER, PRESENTLY, HOW MAY I BE OF ASSISTANCE?

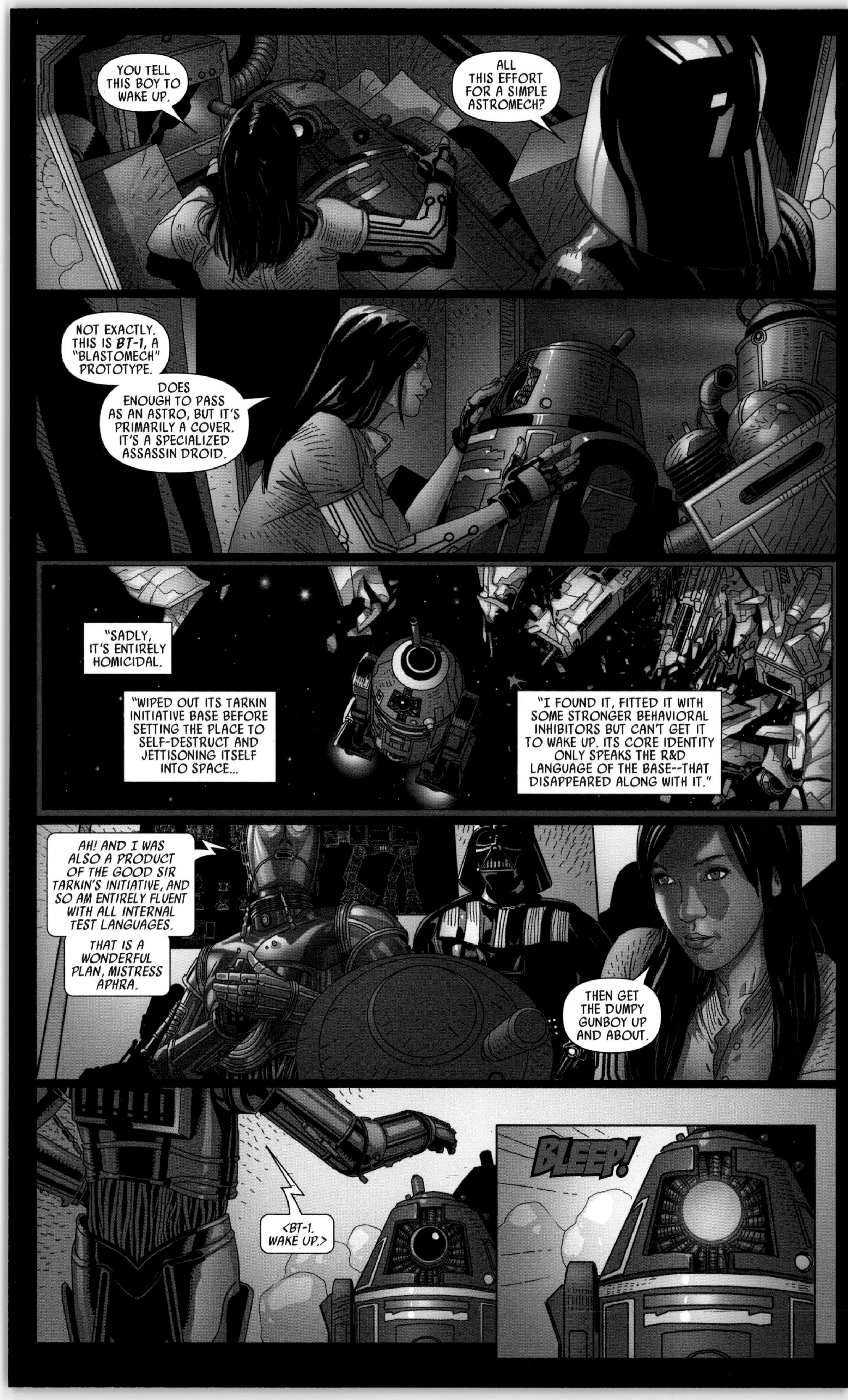
YOU TELL THIS BOY TO WAKE UP.
ALL THIS EFFORT FOR A SIMPLE ASTROMECH?
NOT EXACTLY. THIS IS BT-1, A "BLASTOMECH" PROTOTYPE.
DOES ENOUGH TO PASS AS AN ASTRO, BUT IT'S PRIMARILY A COVER. IT'S A SPECIALIZED ASSASSIN DROID.
"SADLY, IT'S ENTIRELY HOMICIDAL.
"WIPED OUT ITS TARKIN INITIATIVE BASE BEFORE SETTING THE PLACE TO SELF-DESTRUCT AND JETTISONING ITSELF INTO SPACE...
"I FOUND IT, FITTED IT WITH SOME STRONGER BEHAVIORAL INHIBITORS BUT CAN'T GET IT TO WAKE UP. ITS CORE IDENTITY ONLY SPEAKS THE R&D LANGUAGE OF THE BASE--THAT DISAPPEARED ALONG WITH IT."
AH! AND I WAS ALSO A PRODUCT OF THE GOOD SIR TARKIN'S INITIATIVE, AND SO AM ENTIRELY FLUENT WITH ALL INTERNAL TEST LANGUAGES.
THAT IS A WONDERFUL PLAN, MISTRESS APHRA.
THEN GET THE DUMPY GUNBOY UP AND ABOUT.
<BT-1. WAKE UP.>
BLEEP!

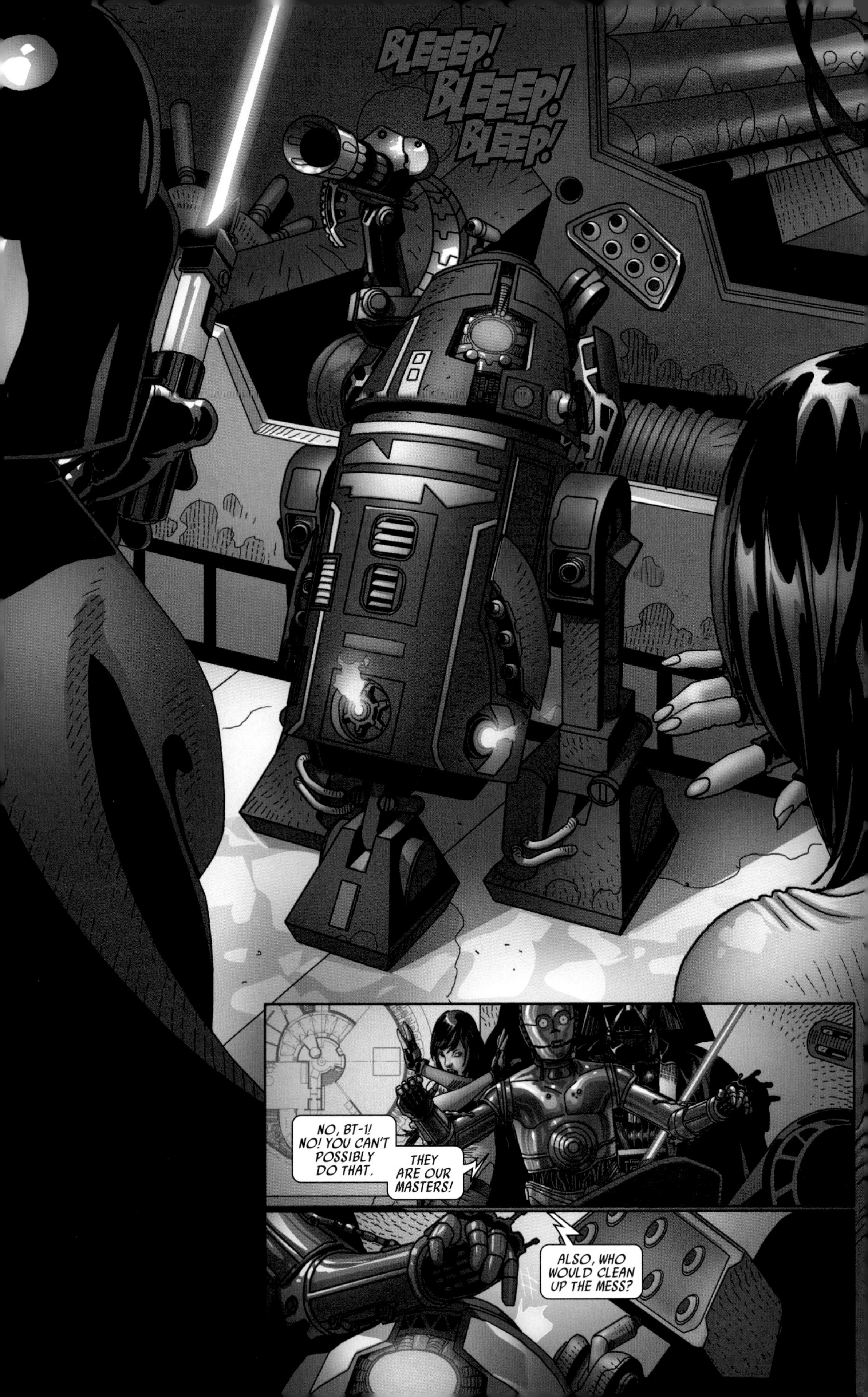
BLEEEP! BLEEEP! BLEEP!
NO, BT-1! NO! YOU CAN'T POSSIBLY DO THAT.
THEY ARE OUR MASTERS!
ALSO, WHO WOULD CLEAN UP THE MESS?

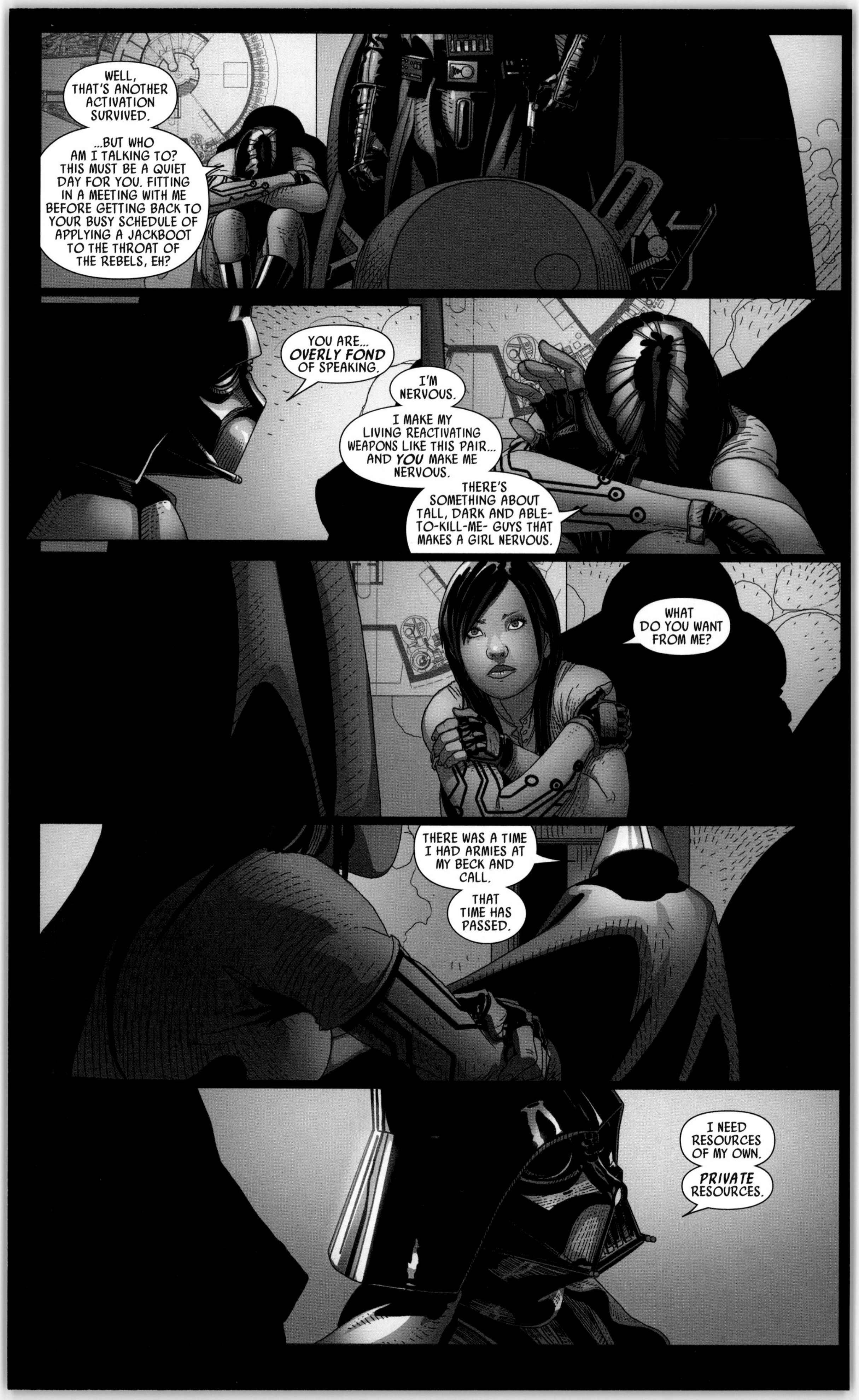
WELL, THAT'S ANOTHER ACTIVATION SURVIVED.
...BUT WHO AM I TALKING TO? THIS MUST BE A QUIET DAY FOR YOU. FITTING IN A MEETING WITH ME BEFORE GETTING BACK TO YOUR BUSY SCHEDULE OF APPLYING A JACKBOOT TO THE THROAT OF THE REBELS, EH?
YOU ARE... *OVERLY FOND* OF SPEAKING.
I'M NERVOUS.
I MAKE MY LIVING REACTIVATING WEAPONS LIKE THIS PAIR... AND *YOU* MAKE ME NERVOUS.
THERE'S SOMETHING ABOUT TALL, DARK AND ABLE-TO-KILL-ME- GUYS THAT MAKES A GIRL NERVOUS.
WHAT DO YOU WANT FROM ME?
THERE WAS A TIME I HAD ARMIES AT MY BECK AND CALL.
THAT TIME HAS PASSED.
I NEED RESOURCES OF MY OWN.
PRIVATE RESOURCES.

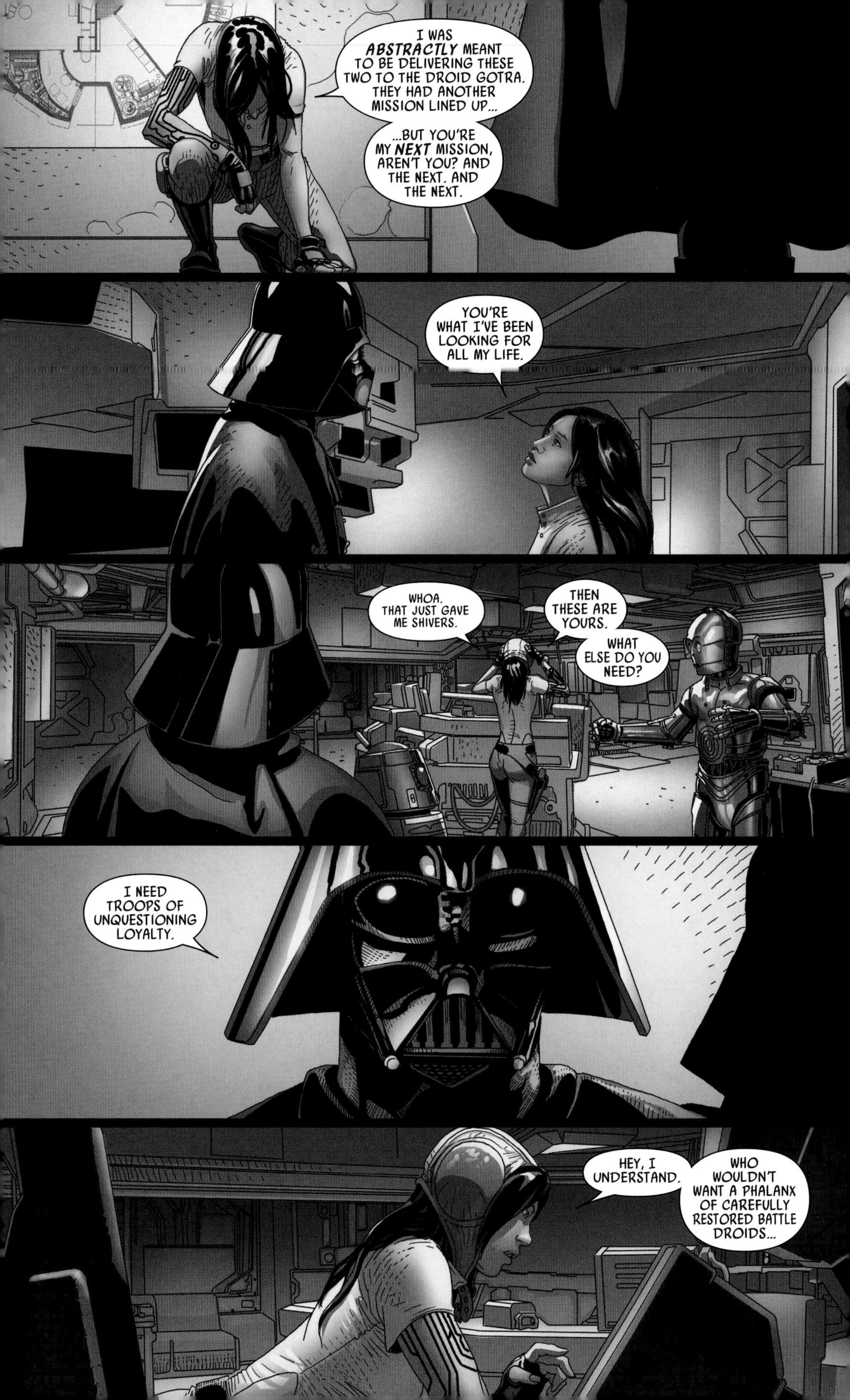

I WAS ABSTRACTLY MEANT TO BE DELIVERING THESE TWO TO THE DROID GOTRA. THEY HAD ANOTHER MISSION LINED UP...
...BUT YOU'RE MY NEXT MISSION, AREN'T YOU? AND THE NEXT. AND THE NEXT.
YOU'RE WHAT I'VE BEEN LOOKING FOR ALL MY LIFE.
WHOA. THAT JUST GAVE ME SHIVERS.
THEN THESE ARE YOURS.
WHAT ELSE DO YOU NEED?
I NEED TROOPS OF UNQUESTIONING LOYALTY.
HEY, I UNDERSTAND.
WHO WOULDN'T WANT A PHALANX OF CAREFULLY RESTORED BATTLE DROIDS...

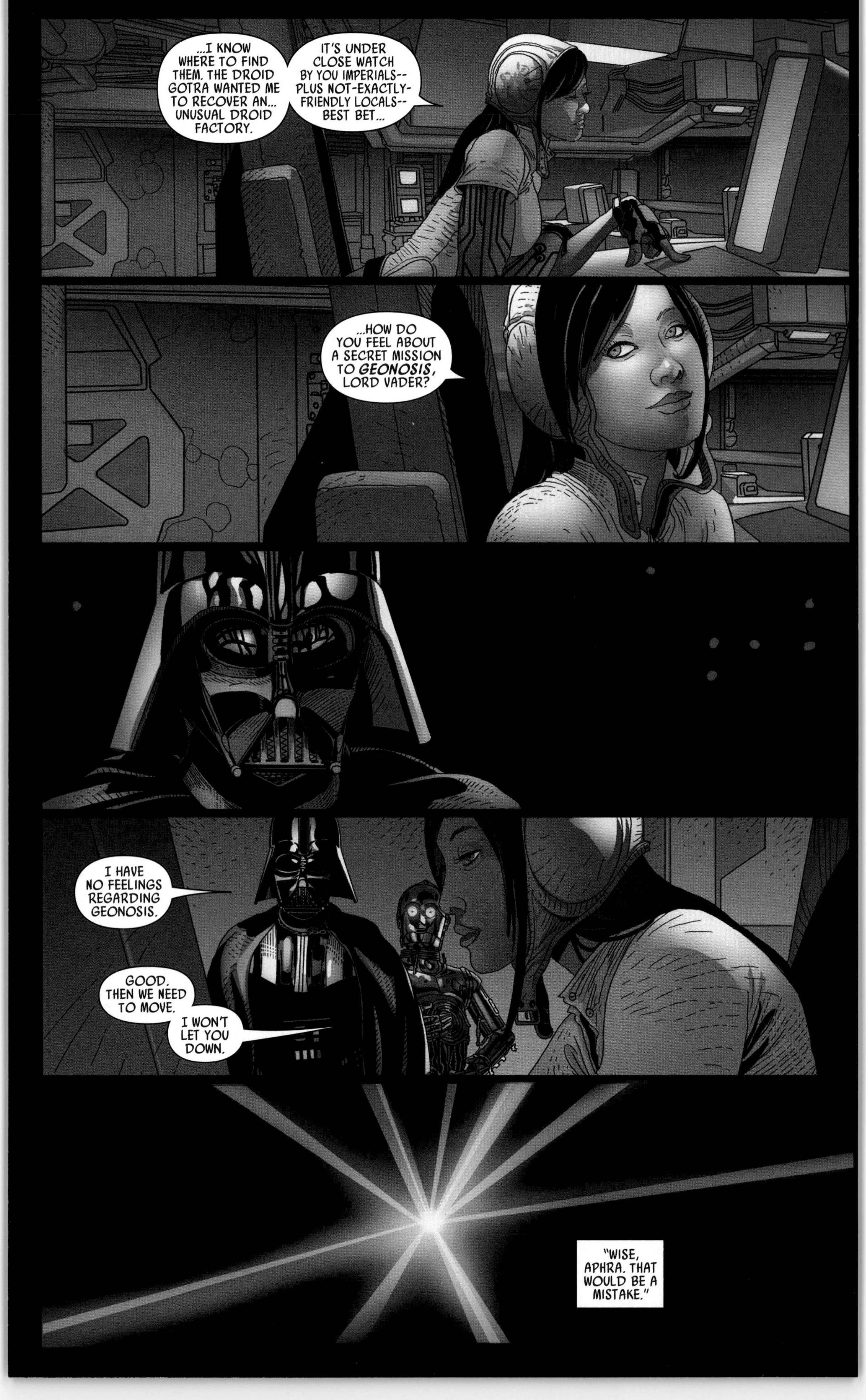
...I KNOW WHERE TO FIND THEM. THE DROID GOTRA WANTED ME TO RECOVER AN... UNUSUAL DROID FACTORY.
IT'S UNDER CLOSE WATCH BY YOU IMPERIALS-- PLUS NOT-EXACTLY-FRIENDLY LOCALS-- BEST BET...
...HOW DO YOU FEEL ABOUT A SECRET MISSION TO GEONOSIS, LORD VADER?
I HAVE NO FEELINGS REGARDING GEONOSIS.
GOOD. THEN WE NEED TO MOVE.
I WON'T LET YOU DOWN.
"WISE, APHRA. THAT WOULD BE A MISTAKE."

STAR WARS®

DARTH VADER

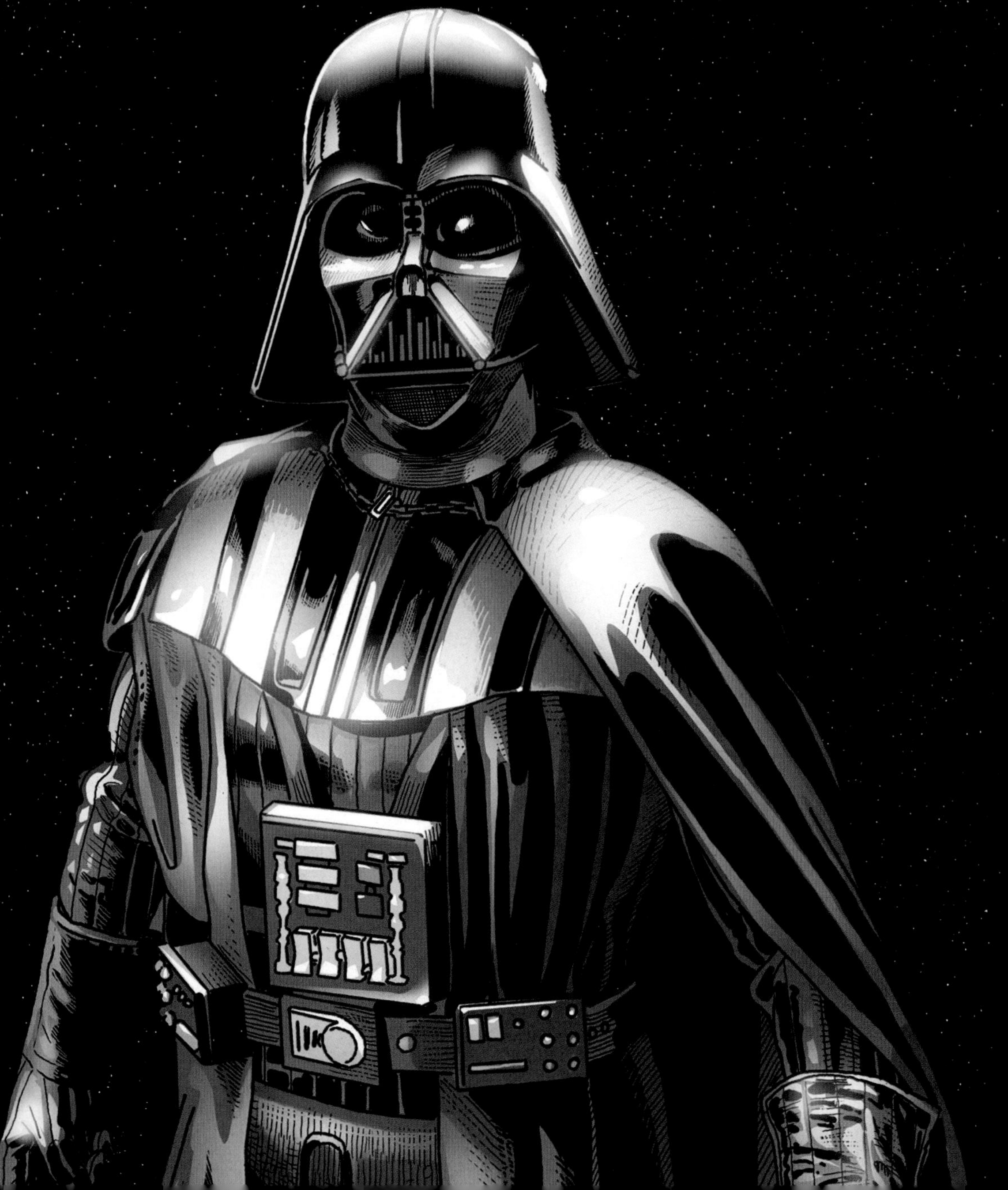

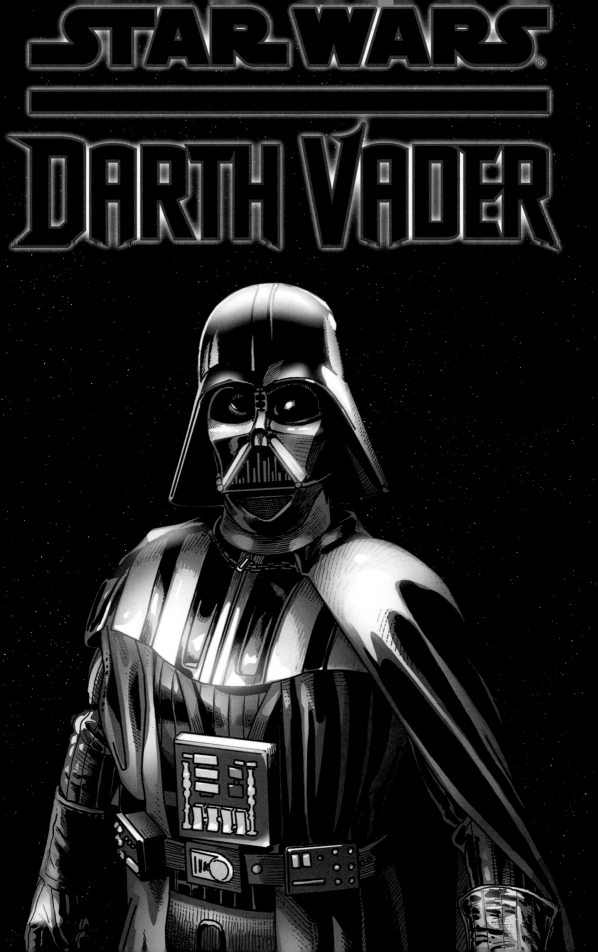

STAR WARS
DARTH VADER

COLLECT THEM ALL!

Set of 6 Hardcover Books ISBN: 978-1-61479-519-3

STAR WARS
STAR WARS
DARTH VADER
VADER: VOLUME 1
GILLEN LARROCA DELGADO

Hardcover Book ISBN
978-1-61479-520-9

STAR WARS
STAR WARS
DARTH VADER
VADER: VOLUME 2
GILLEN LARROCA DELGADO

Hardcover Book ISBN
978-1-61479-521-6

STAR WARS
STAR WARS
DARTH VADER
VADER: VOLUME 3
GILLEN LARROCA DELGADO

Hardcover Book ISBN
978-1-61479-522-3

STAR WARS
STAR WARS
DARTH VADER
VADER: VOLUME 4
GILLEN LARROCA DELGADO

Hardcover Book ISBN
978-1-61479-523-0

STAR WARS
STAR WARS
DARTH VADER
VADER: VOLUME 5
GILLEN LARROCA DELGADO

Hardcover Book ISBN
978-1-61479-524-7

STAR WARS
STAR WARS
DARTH VADER
VADER: VOLUME 6
GILLEN LARROCA DELGADO

Hardcover Book ISBN
978-1-61479-525-4

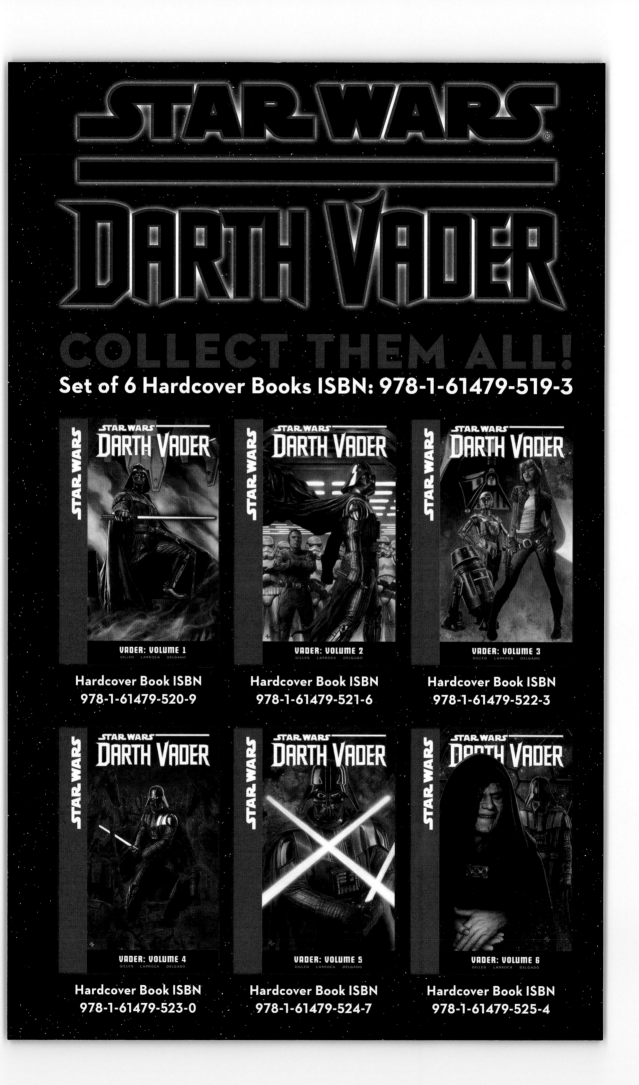